HOCUS POCUS HOTEL

Hocus Pocus Hotel is published by Stone Arch Books
A Capstone Imprint
1710 Roe Crest Dr.
North Mankato, Minnesota 56003
www.capstonepub.com

Designed by Kay Fraser
Photo credits: Shutterstock

Library of Congress Cataloging-in-Publication Data
Dahl, Michael.
To catch a ghost / by Michael Dahl ; illustrated by Lisa Weber.
p. cm. -- (Hocus pocus hotel)
Summary: Tyler Yu, school bully, is convinced that there is a
ghost stealing things at Abracadabra Hotel, and he enlists the help
of Charlie Hitchcock to solve the mystery.
ISBN 978-1-4342-4100-9 (library binding)
1. Magicians--Juvenile fiction. 2. Magic tricks--Juvenile fiction.
3. Hotels--Juvenile fiction. [1. Mystery and detective stories. 2.
Magic tricks--Fiction. 3. Hotels, motels, etc.--Fiction.] I. Weber,
Lisa K., ill. II. Title.

PZ7.D15134To 2012

813.6--dc23   2012000329

Printed in the United States of America
in North Mankato, Minnesota.
042012   006682CGF12

To Catch a Ghost

BY MICHAEL DAHL

ILLUSTRATED BY LISA K. WEBER

STONE ARCH BOOKS™
a capstone imprint

3 THE ABRACADABRA HOTEL

Table of

Contents

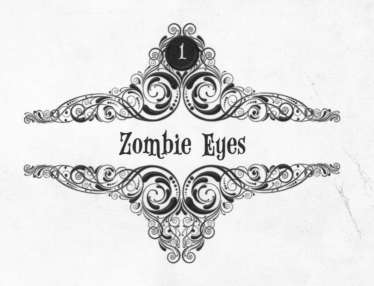

Zombie Eyes

Charlie Hitchcock was the smartest kid at Blackstone Middle School.

Tyler Yu was the most feared, because of his temper, his muscles, and the scowl he always wore.

Although they were both in the seventh grade, they had never spoken to each other at school. But together, they had solved an impossible mystery a few days ago.

This afternoon, they stood once more in the vast, shadowy lobby of the Abracadabra Hotel, where Tyler lived with his parents. They were back at the Abracadabra to solve another mystery: Tyler was sure the hotel was being haunted by a ghost.

Outside the building, an October thunderstorm crashed and boomed. Lighting flashed, lighting up the giant painting that hung on the lobby wall. The man in the painting was a magician, Abracadabra himself, the founder of the hotel. He was tall and skinny, with a thin black mustache ending in two enormous spirals. The lightning reflected off his dark shiny eyes.

Zombie eyes, thought Charlie.

Tyler glanced over and asked, "You're not spooked, are you, Hitch?"

Charlie put his hands in his pockets. "Oh no," he said, rolling his eyes. "I'm standing in an empty lobby in a creepy hotel in the middle of a thunderstorm, and you just told me that there's a ghost floating around here. Why should I be spooked?" he said, rolling his eyes.

He turned and looked out the hotel's glass doors. Sheets of rain fell on the street and sidewalk. "I'm going to get soaked when I go home," he said.

"When did you tell your parents you'd be home?" asked Tyler.

"Uh, I didn't say," Charlie said.

"Good," said Tyler. "Come on. I'll show you the room where the ghost struck first."

"But why do you think it's a ghost?" asked Charlie. "I mean, did someone see a spirit or something?"

"It's because of the voice," said Tyler.

"Voice?" Charlie repeated. Without meaning to, he shivered. He hoped Tyler didn't notice.

"And because of stuff disappearing," said Ty. "And because of what Mr. Thursday said."

Why did I let myself get dragged into another mystery with Ty? wondered Charlie. Because it was another puzzle? Because he was afraid Tyler would pound him into the dirt if he didn't help him?

"My mom doesn't believe in ghosts," said Ty. "She thinks I'm making up excuses for not wanting to go up to the ninth floor. And she says if I don't find the missing stuff, it will come out of my pay."

Charlie knew what no pay would mean. If Tyler didn't get paid, he couldn't buy the dirt bike he was saving up for. A Tezuki Slamhammer 750, Edition 6, in cherry-pop lightning red.

Tyler had once shown Charlie a picture of the bike. It was super cool, if you were into that sort of thing. But making you pay for things that had disappeared, when it wasn't your fault — that didn't seem fair.

"What does your dad think about the ghost?" Charlie asked.

"He doesn't go up to the ninth floor either," said Ty. "Especially since he heard the voice."

Thunder crashed and Charlie jumped. Tyler noticed, but he didn't say anything. He didn't even grin. Instead, he simply said, "Come on, Hitch."

The taller, dark-haired boy led the way across the lobby, past tall marble columns and tall potted palm trees. A row of elevators lined the back wall. Their shiny metal doors shone like gold.

The elevator car on the far left was open. Inside stood a thin, elderly man in a maroon-and-black uniform. He smiled a wrinkly smile and waved his hand at the boys.

"Dang!" said Ty. "Wait here. I have to grab the passkey." He spun around and sprinted toward the lobby desk.

"Hey, take my backpack and put it behind the counter," said Charlie.

"I'm not your assistant," said Tyler. As he rushed away, his shoes made wet prints in the thick, blood-red carpet.

"Master Yu is always in a hurry," said the old man. His name was Brack, and he was the hotel's only elevator operator.

"He knows I can't stay that long," said Charlie.

"Are you helping him solve another mystery?" asked Brack.

Charlie swung his backpack onto one shoulder. "I like puzzles," he said. "Well, actually, I hate puzzles. They bug me until I figure out the answer."

Brack nodded thoughtfully. "Then prepare to be bugged," he said. "Our hotel is full of puzzles. Riddles and mysteries are built in the walls."

No kidding, Charlie thought.

Just then, Tyler appeared back at the elevator, breathing hard. "Got it," he said, holding up the key. "Ninth floor, Brack."

Thunder shook the building. "Hey, Mr. Brack," said Charlie. "You don't believe in ghosts, right?"

"Believe in them?" replied Brack. "Of course I do. Why, I've seen them." He pushed a button, the golden doors shut, and the elevator car shot upward.

Haunted Bathtubs

The boys were stunned. "You saw a ghost?" said Tyler.

Brack nodded. The elevator car hummed and shuddered as it rose toward the ninth floor.

"Where did you see it?" asked Charlie.

"In the elevator," answered Brack. He pointed a finger toward the shining gold doors. "I had just dropped off a customer on twelve, and was coming back down to the lobby. And then I saw Abracadabra the magician standing right there, staring at me."

The magician from the painting, thought Charlie. Abracadabra, the founder of the building, had lived there long ago.

"Did he say anything?" asked Charlie in a whisper.

"Not a syllable," said Brack sadly. "And when I reached the lobby, he disappeared."

"Wow," said Tyler.

"But I've seen him many times since," added Brack.

"On the ninth floor?" asked Ty.

"On many floors," said the elevator operator.

The elevator stopped. Charlie watched his and Ty's reflections, with their mouths hanging open, disappear as the doors slid open. A dark hallway lay beyond.

"You don't have to leave right away, Brack," said Ty. "We won't be long."

"I'll wait as long as I can, Master Yu," said the older man. "But if I hear someone else ring the bell, I'll have to go."

Tyler nodded. He and Charlie started down the hallway, leaving the elevator operator behind. "It's Mr. Thursday's room," said Ty. "Just around the corner: 909."

At the first door around the corner, Tyler shoved the passkey into the lock.

"Don't you knock first?" asked Charlie.

"Relax," said Tyler. "We moved him to a different room after the ghost thing happened. It was easy since he didn't have any luggage. The airline lost it or something."

"Oh," said Charlie.

After stepping inside, Tyler flipped on a light. "The bathroom's over here," he said.

The bathroom was as big as Charlie's bedroom. Marble counters, fancy mirrors, a shaggy white rug, and a huge bathtub fit inside, and there was plenty of room left over.

"Notice anything missing?" asked Tyler, crossing his arms.

"Yes," said Charlie. He stared at the bare curtain rod that hung around the clawfoot tub. "The shower curtain. That's what's missing."

"Exactly," said Tyler. "The same night Mr. Thursday checked in, he heard a noise in the middle of the night."

"What kind of noise?" Charlie asked.

Tyler shrugged. "He wasn't sure, really," he said. "He said that at first he thought it was a fire. Then as he listened some more, he said it sounded like someone crumpling up paper. And it was coming from the bathroom."

Creepy, thought Charlie.

"Creepy, huh?" said Tyler. "And when he got up to look, he switched on the light, but no one was there. And the shower curtain was gone."

"The room door was locked?" asked Charlie.

Tyler nodded. "From the inside."

"Had he seen the curtain before he went to bed?" asked Charlie.

"Yes," said Ty. "He said he took a shower when he first got in. Then he went downstairs and had dinner."

"Ah, and that's when the curtain was stolen!" said Charlie. "While he was at dinner!"

"Uh, no," said Tyler. "When he got back to the room, he brushed his teeth before he went to bed. The curtain was still there."

"Why would someone want a shower curtain?" said Charlie.

"Especially a ghost," added Tyler. "They don't need to take showers."

"He didn't take a shower," said Charlie, "he took a shower curtain. And I still don't see why you think it's a ghost."

"Who else could get into a locked room?" Tyler asked, throwing up his hands. "Who else could remove a solid shower curtain without opening the door?"

"Hmm. Maybe Mr. Thursday did it himself and he's lying," said Charlie.

"I thought of that," said Tyler. "I'm not stupid. I searched the room. I even looked everywhere. It wasn't here."

Maybe he threw it out the window, Charlie thought. *But that doesn't make sense. Why would anyone do that?*

"And he couldn't have thrown it out the window, because the room windows don't open," said Tyler.

Charlie stared at him. "How did you know I was thinking about that?" he asked.

"I saw you glance at the window with a funny look on your mug," said Tyler.

"Oh," Charlie said, blushing.

Ty went on, "And the first time I came in here, that's what I thought too." A smirk spread across his face. "I'm not so dumb after all, am I?"

"I never said you were," said Charlie. In fact, he thought Tyler was pretty smart. Tyler just never showed he had brains at school. He only showed off his big arms and fists.

Tyler ran a hand through his spiky black hair. "It's crazy," he said. "I just don't get it. Oh, and by the way, this isn't the only room where the shower curtain disappeared."

Tyler led Charlie to five more rooms on the same floor, opening each one with the hotel's passkey. In each one, the shower curtain was missing. Only the metal rings that once held them in place still dangled on the curtain rods.

"The maids found these," said Tyler. "They always check out the rooms even if no one has used them. Just to make sure everything is in place. And, get this, none of these rooms has had a guest in it for over a week. They've all been empty. And the cleaning people swore the shower curtains were still there when they cleaned the rooms."

"They couldn't have made a mistake?" asked Charlie.

"No way," said Tyler. "The cleaning crew has a checklist for each room. If anything is missing, they have to report it. My mom's a real stickler for being organized and clean."

"Six rooms without shower curtains," said Charlie.

"There's other stuff missing too," said Tyler. "Okay, come on. Now we need to go downstairs."

"There could be more than one ghost," said Charlie.

Suddenly, they both froze. A moan echoed through the dim hallway.

"There it is!" whispered Tyler. "The voice."

Mr. Ken

A name was being called out over and over. "Mister Ken . . . Mister Ken . . ."

The voice was soft, but clear. "See what I mean?" said Tyler quietly.

He motioned for Charlie to walk down the corridor with him. Even as they tiptoed past door after door, the voice seemed to follow them.

Charlie tapped Ty's back and whispered, "Where's it coming from?"

Tyler shook his head. "I can't tell. I've put my ears to the doors on this floor, but it isn't coming from inside anywhere. It's out here, in the hall."

"Mister Ken . . . Mister Ken . . ." The voice sounded angry. When it wasn't speaking the man's name, it was merely moaning.

"You go down that hall," said Tyler, pointing. "I'll go down this way."

Charlie nodded and headed down the hallway. He wished he had a flashlight. Even with flashes of lightning through the hall windows, it was hard to see.

The ancient wallpaper was decorated with big black flowers.

Lilies? wondered Charlie.

The carpet was a deep green. The hall lamps were small and old-fashioned, dim and covered with thick red shades.

It reminded Charlie of walking through a funhouse. Or a creepy hotel in a scary movie. He half expected to see ghostly kids each time he turned a corner. But, except for Tyler, he was the only other person walking the halls.

Neither of them saw a ghost or a moving shadow or a floating orb of light. Separately, they made a circuit of all the halls on the ninth floor.

They passed the row of elevators twice (Mr. Brack was gone by then). And though the voice was equally clear throughout the hallways, they still couldn't tell where it was coming from.

For a while, Charlie thought that Ty was playing a trick on him.

Firstly, Charlie didn't believe in ghosts, so he had a hard time believing that the biggest bully in school did.

Secondly, he could easily imagine Tyler telling his buddies how he had pranked Charlie and freaked him out.

But after several minutes of prowling the halls, Charlie could tell that Ty was nervous too. Every time they passed each other, Tyler would ask, "Anything?"

Charlie would shake his head and say, "You?" Tyler would shake his head. And the two would keep walking.

Charlie did notice that the voice seemed to change volume as he walked. It would grow softer and then louder as he walked down a hall. If he retraced his steps to where the sound had been soft, it grew softer once more.

Weird, thought Charlie.

Charlie noticed something else. A second sound. It was softer than the mysterious voice, but always there in the background. A tinkling sound, like a tiny silver bell.

Suddenly, the voice grew rougher, heavier. There was a loud bang.

The voice cried out one more time, and then — silence.

"Wow," said Tyler, walking up to Charlie.

"So, who's this Mister Ken guy?" asked Charlie.

"Beats me," said Ty. "A magician, maybe? They always call themselves Mister this or Mister that. I wonder if he used to live here a long time ago and maybe died in the hotel."

"Or maybe it's the ghost of Abracadabra," added Charlie.

"It would make sense for him to haunt the hotel he built," said Ty. "Let's ask Brack. He knows everything about this place."

"Maybe there's a record of accidents that happened here," said Charlie. "We could Google it, I bet."

He pushed the button for an elevator, but when the next one came, it was not Brack's. "No problem," said Tyler. "We need to go back downstairs anyway."

As they stepped inside the elevator, Charlie thought about the ghost that had shown itself to the elderly operator. Something about Brack's story didn't sound right.

The Missing

When they reached the first-floor lobby,
Tyler led Charlie past the front desk and
down a broad flight of steps.

At the bottom, they walked through
several more corridors and finally came to a
huge room with a shiny wooden floor.

"You have a bowling alley down here?" exclaimed Charlie. His voice echoed in the large, empty space.

"Yup," said Tyler. "With nine lanes. But it's closed now because of the ghost."

"Don't tell me he stole the bowling balls," said Charlie.

"No, the pins," Tyler said. "Not all of them. Just nine. One from each alley."

"This is getting weirder by the minute," said Charlie.

"And it's not over," said Ty.

As he led Charlie back toward the marble steps, they passed another door. Actually, it was a set of double doors. Charlie noticed that the carved wooden doors were each decorated with a face. One face was smiling, and one was frowning.

"What's that?" Charlie asked.

"Oh, that's the old theater," said Tyler, sounding bored.

Charlie darted over and peered inside the doors. It was another huge room, bigger than the bowling alley. Rows of red velvet seats faced a large stage. The stage curtains looked about a mile high. They were pulled to the sides so that the shiny wooden floor of the stage could be clearly seen.

Charlie rubbed his hand along the back of one of the theater chairs. "Cool," he whispered.

"No one's used this place for years," said Tyler. "This is where they used to have the old magic shows. Come on, let's go."

He led Charlie back up the stairs and into the hotel's main floor restaurant, the Top Hat.

Several of the tables and booths were already filled with hungry guests. At the back of the dining area was the kitchen. Warm air and chattering voices greeted the boys as they passed through the kitchen's swinging doors.

"Hey, Dad!" yelled Ty.

A tall man wearing a tall white chef's hat hurried over to meet him.

"Tyler, you shouldn't be back here," said Mr. Yu. "Only cooks and waiters."

"I know, I know," said Tyler.

"Who's this?" asked his father, gesturing toward Charlie. "Your friend from school?"

"Yeah, this is Hitch," said Ty. "He's here because he's interested in the ghost."

"Ah," said his father, nodding his head. "Our phantom friend."

Charlie noticed that the older Yu had the same eyes as his son. But his face was much friendlier.

Tyler must get his scowl from his mom, thought Charlie.

"Tell him what the ghost took from your kitchen, Dad," said Tyler.

"I don't know if it was a ghost," said Mr. Yu, smiling. "But someone took a half dozen of my best serving spoons."

"The big kind," added Tyler. "You know, for scooping out stuff."

"We run a tight ship here at the Top Hat," said Mr. Yu. "Every pot, pan, plate, and utensil is accounted for. I really can't understand why anyone would want serving spoons."

"Are they valuable?" asked Charlie.

"Well, they are old," admitted Mr. Yu. "And I'm sure they're genuine silver. They came with the original silverware from the hotel's first restaurant."

"Think they're worth a hundred bucks, Dad?" asked Tyler.

"Probably more," said Mr. Yu, nodding. "Now, I really need to get back to my customers. We're serving one of my specialties tonight, Flambeau de Chesterton. I have to make sure I don't set off the fire alarm like I did last time. You boys have fun."

As they returned to the lobby, Charlie stopped asked, "Why do you think a ghost stole the serving spoons?"

"Not so loud," whispered Tyler. "I don't want the guests to hear. It's bad for business."

He grabbed Charlie by the collar and pulled him into a shadowy corner, where they were surrounded by potted palms and giant ceramic vases.

"There's no one around," said Charlie, readjusting his collar.

"Yeah, but that lobby echoes," said Tyler. He shrugged. "My family has a reputation to think about here."

"So tell me why you think —" Charlie began.

"Yeah, yeah, the ghost," said Tyler. "Definitely took the spoons. And I think so because it all happened the same night. After Mr. Thursday called us upstairs about the shower curtain, that same night, my dad noticed his spoons were gone. And later, my mom got complaints from some of the guests that the bowling pins were missing downstairs."

"That is weird," said Charlie.

"No kidding," said Tyler. "This is why you need to solve the mystery. And it better be quick, before something else disappears."

Just then, a hand reached out from behind one of the giant vases.

Finding the Key

Tyler jumped as the hand grabbed him.

"Where's my key?" came a voice.

The mysterious hand grabbed Tyler's shirt
even tighter.

Charlie saw that it was attached to an
arm, then a shoulder, then an entire body of
a teenage boy with long blond hair.

The older boy was wearing a dark maroon suit and a gold name badge.

"Don't do that!" said Tyler. He shook the guy's hand away.

"Sorry, man," said the teenager. "I need my passkey back." He turned and looked at Charlie. "Who are you?"

Charlie began, "I'm —"

"He's Hitch," said Tyler. "And here's your stupid passkey." He handed it to the blond guy, who shoved it in his pocket.

"Your mom was looking for it," said the blond guy. "And I don't want to lose it like last time."

"You lost it?" Charlie asked.

The blond guy turned to Tyler. "Who is this kid?" he asked. "And why does he care about my stupid passkey?"

"I'm, uh, writing a report on the hotel for school," said Charlie. "Who are you?"

"Rocky," said the guy. "I work the front desk."

"He and Annie switch off," explained Tyler.

"When did you lose the key?" Charlie asked.

"I didn't really lose it," said Rocky. "I just misplaced it. I was checking people in and I had a lot on my mind. I couldn't find the key, but when I looked again a little later, there it was on the floor. Must have dropped it. Anyway, why do you care when I lost it?"

"Don't you have work to do?" asked Tyler.

"Nice talking to you too, Ty," said Rocky. He pushed his long hair behind his ears and walked back toward the desk.

"Well, that could explain our ghost," said Charlie.

"What could explain the ghost? Rocky?" asked Tyler.

"No, not Rocky. The passkey," said Charlie. "Rocky said he was missing it for a little while, right? So while it was gone, someone could have used it to get into the rooms on the ninth floor and steal the shower curtains."

"You're right," said Tyler.

"And does the passkey let you into the bowling alley and the kitchen?" asked Charlie.

"Yeah. It unlocks every door in the hotel," said Tyler.

"So that's how the thief did it," said Charlie.

"But how could you steal a key right in front of someone?" asked Tyler. "Rocky's not that smart, but he does notice things. He knew you and I were over here behind these plants and vases."

"Right," Charlie said. "That's why I think it had to be a magician."

"Why?" Tyler asked.

"Magicians use the trick I'm thinking of all the time," said Charlie. "It's called palming. It's how they can hide an object in their hands, right under your nose. Or they distract you, make you look at something else, while they put the object in their pocket."

"Hmm," said Tyler.

He strode across the lobby and stopped at the front desk. Rocky was busy working at a computer.

"PALMING"

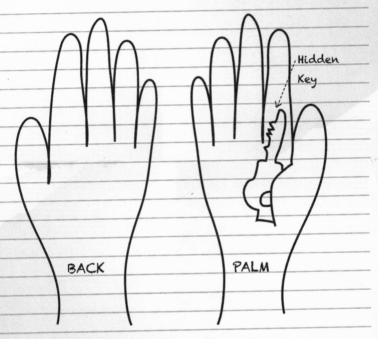

Hidden Key

BACK   PALM

A magician palms, or hides an object in the palm
of his hand, by grabbing onto it with the fatty
part of his thumb.

"Hey, Rock," said Tyler. "The day you couldn't find that key, were there lots of people checking in?"

"I'm busy here, Ty," said Rocky.

"Just tell me what you dropped on the floor that day," said Tyler.

"Just someone's credit card and . . . hey, how did you know I dropped something?" Rocky asked, turning from the computer.

"Elementary," said Tyler, with a smirk. "Whose card was it?'

"And when did all this happen?" added Charlie.

Rocky thought for a moment. He brushed the hair out of his eyes and said, "It was Thursday."

Then Charlie asked, "And were any of those people you checked in named Ken?"

"You're starting to bug me, kid," said Rocky.

"Hey, can you answer his question or not?" said Tyler.

Rocky frowned and looked quickly at his computer screen. "Nope, no Ken. Hey, no Ken do. Get it? You asked if I could answer his question, and I said, 'No Ken do.' Ha."

"You're a comedian," said Tyler. "Come on," he told Charlie.

The two boys walked away from the counter. Tyler shook and head and shoved his hands into the back pockets of his jeans.

"What a weirdo," he mumbled. "Well, now what do we do?"

This puzzle was more bizarre than the last one Charlie had helped Tyler solve. A ghost, a wavering voice, missing bowling pins, spoons, and shower curtains.

Or maybe not exactly shower curtains, Charlie thought. There was something he had seen in Mr. Thursday's bathroom that he hadn't seen in the others Tyler had showed him.

And there was something else. The weirdest thing was that Charlie was sure there was a phantom cleaner in the hotel. Things were being cleaned without anyone else realizing it.

Suddenly, grunts echoed through the lobby. Charlie turned and saw a couple of men walk toward the counter where Rocky was working. Rain dripped from their clothes and their shoes.

The men had thick necks and broad shoulders, but they were struggling with two huge suitcases. They set them down by Rocky, then took out handkerchiefs and wiped their foreheads.

"We got one more," said one of the
men. He jerked his thumb over his shoulder
toward the front door. Charlie could see an
empty taxi sitting by the curb.

Charlie looked at the suitcases again.
Things were starting to make sense to him.

"I think we need to go back up to
the ninth floor," said Charlie. "There's
something else missing from the bathroom
in Room 909."

The Echo

"I don't hear the voice," said Tyler.

"Me either," Charlie said. "Just wait."

They were walking through the hallways again on the ninth floor.

When they reached Room 909, Tyler unlocked the door with the passkey.

He'd grabbed it while Rocky was busy with the heavy suitcases that had just arrived.

"Okay, Hitch," said Tyler. "What's the deal with Mr. Thursday's bathroom?"

"Look at the curtain rod," said Charlie. "See anything?"

"Uh, no," replied Tyler. "I already told you the ghost, or whoever, stole the shower curtains."

"Right," said Charlie. "But I remember something else from the other bathrooms. Since I have acute visual memory, I remember . . ."

"Yeah, yeah, I know," said Tyler, with a frown. "You remember everything you see."

"And it doesn't match this room," Charlie pointed out.

Tyler frowned, but he took off and ran to one of the other hotel rooms. Charlie followed as Tyler rushed inside the other room and disappeared into the bathroom. "Wow!" came his voice.

"See it?" asked Charlie.

Tyler walked slowly out of the second bathroom and stared at Charlie. "You did it again, Hitch," he said. "This bathroom has the curtain rings still attached."

"They all do," said Charlie. "Except for the curtain rod in Mr. Thursday's bathroom. The shower curtains and the rings are missing."

"But why?" asked Tyler. "What's the difference?"

"Let's see, there are about twelve or so rings on each rod," Charlie said thoughtfully. "Someone wanted those rings."

"They're not valuable," said Tyler. "Just made out of metal."

Ooooooh-ooooooohhhhhh!

The boys stared at each other. The voice had returned.

"This guy is starting to tick me off," growled Tyler. He rushed out of the room and strode down the hallway. "Where are you?" he called out. "What's your problem?!"

Charlie followed him, listening closely to the phantom sound. "Mister Ken . . . ahhhh . . . uhhh . . . Mister Ken . . ." The moan echoed through the hall.

"Wait here," said Charlie. He rushed back to the hallway where he had earlier noticed the ghost's voice growing softer. Yes, it was still soft in that area. Charlie walked down the hall until the voice seemed louder again.

There has to be a logical explanation, he thought.

He dropped his backpack onto the carpet and knelt down. He fished through one of the pockets to find his notebook and a pen. He wanted to write down all the clues they had discovered so far.

Then he noticed something. When he was kneeling down on the floor, the sound was louder.

What is going on? he thought. Staying on his knees, he crawled to one side of the hall. No, the sound was normal. Then he crawled to the other side. The voice was louder.

Charlie stared at the dark wall. The wallpaper design of big black flowers stretched all the way to the floor. But in the dim light, Charlie could see that there was a small vent disguised in the black petals.

He pressed an ear to the vent and heard the ghostly voice loud and clear.

He sat up and called out, "Hey, Tyler! Come here!"

Tyler rushed into the hall. "You saw it?" he asked.

Charlie shook his head. "No," he said, "but I heard it." He pointed at the vent. Tyler bent down and listened closely. They both heard Mister Ken's name cried out again.

"I know where it's coming from," Tyler said suddenly.

"Where?" Charlie asked.

Tyler shuddered and said, "The basement!"

Behind the Boilers

On the way down in the elevator — this time it was Brack's — Charlie made a list on his notepad of the clues and questions they had.

"You have the hunter's gleam in your eye, Master Hitchcock," said Brack. "Do I detect that you have solved the puzzle?"

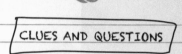

CLUES AND QUESTIONS

1. Missing spoons, curtain rings, bowling pins → (why would one person want all three of these objects?)

2. Other shower curtains missing on Floor 9 ↳ EXTREMELY WEIRD

3. A ghostly voice in the vent

4. Who (or what) is Mister Ken?

5. The lost passkey ??

6. Heavy luggage turning up at the counter

"He'd better have solved it," muttered Tyler.

Charlie grinned and told Brack, "Well, I've solved at least part of it."

Brack leaned in to look at Charlie's list. "So you have juggled all your clues and evidence together," he said, "and that's why you are traveling to the basement?"

"We always end up in the basement," said Tyler.

"But the mystery was already solved upstairs on the ninth floor," said Charlie. "Down here, we'll find out who's behind the mystery."

The elevator stopped and the doors slid open.

"Good luck," said Brack. "I hope your solution turns tragedy into comedy."

As the elevator doors closed behind them, Tyler looked down at Charlie and said, "That guy is always saying weird stuff."

Weird, but full of clues, thought Charlie. *Tragedy and comedy?*

"I think he's pretty smart," Charlie said, raising an eyebrow. "Anyway, where should we go?"

Tyler shrugged and pointed. "This way," he said. "Follow the pipes."

Long metal ducts snaked across the ceilings. As they walked deeper into the basement, more and more of the ducts appeared from different directions.

The ducts connected and joined together, forming even bigger pipes, all running in the same direction. All of the pipes passed through a wall near a door labeled BOILER ROOM in thick, dark letters.

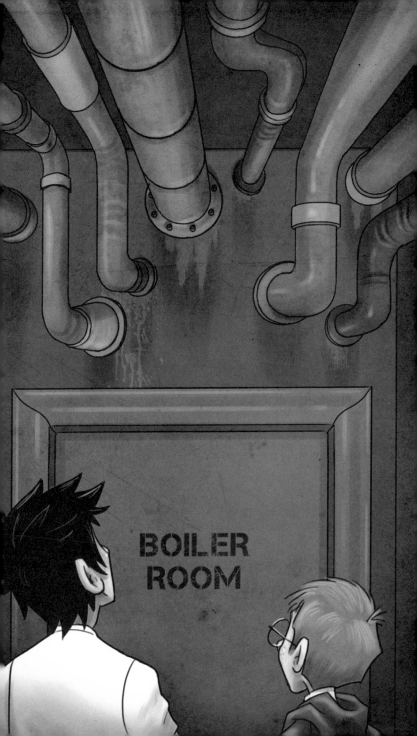

When the boys opened the heavy orange metal door, Tyler and Charlie were met by a blast of thick, warm air.

All the ducts entered this room. Half of them flowed into the dozen metal boilers. The boilers heated air. Then the air was carried by the other ducts to the vents on all the hotel's floors.

"If someone could be heard through that vent upstairs," whispered Tyler, "then they must be somewhere in this room. They have to be."

Then Charlie gasped. He grabbed Tyler's arm. "Look! Over there!" he said.

A man's shadow covered one of the room's cement walls. His hands fluttered up and down in a strange way, as if he were brushing aside spider webs. Or as if he were a magician casting a spell.

His hands stopped.

"Mister Ken," they heard him say. Then the man's shadow disappeared.

Mr. Thursday

"Hurry!" said Tyler. "Before he disappears!"

The boys dashed around the row of boilers.

A young man turned abruptly, a surprised look on his face.

He was surrounded by nine bowling pins. A heap of metal spoons and rings was lying at his feet. Beyond him lay a neatly folded shower curtain.

"Mr. Thursday! You're the ghost!" accused Tyler angrily.

"Ghost?" repeated the man. "What are you talking about?"

"He's not a ghost," said Charlie. "He's a juggler."

"Juggler?" repeated Tyler.

The man bowed toward them. "Thursday the Master Thrower," said the juggler. "And I'm sorry about taking these things. But I had to practice."

"And your luggage was lost by the airlines," said Charlie. "Along with your usual props, like bowling pins, juggling rings, and metal rods."

"Exactly," said Mr. Thursday. "I just borrowed these items to use until mine turned up. I always planned to return them. I even folded the shower curtain!"

He pointed at the shower curtain, which was indeed folded up.

"Your luggage just got here," said Charlie. "We saw it up in the lobby."

"Slow down, you two," Tyler said. "What's going on?"

"He's another performer," explained Charlie. "Like the magicians who live here. And just like any performer, he has to practice every single day."

"But why do you practice down here?" asked Tyler.

"Because the ceiling's high enough," said Mr. Thursday.

"So we were hearing you practice through the vents," said Tyler. "Who is this Mister Ken guy?"

"Mister Ken?" Thursday said. "Who's that?"

Charlie smiled. "He wasn't saying Mister Ken," he said. "We just thought he was. I finally figured it out when I realized what all three objects had in common."

"What do you mean?" Tyler asked. "What do they have in common?"

Charlie explained, "I was thinking, 'What would someone use rings, spoons, and bowling pins for?' Then I thought, 'Of course! Juggling!' Then I realized that what we were hearing was Mr. Thursday rehearsing his act."

"I still don't get it. What does that have to do with Mister Ken?" Tyler asked.

Charlie smiled again. "There is no Mister Ken," he said. "Whenever he dropped a spoon or ring or pin, he would say to himself, 'Missed again, missed again.'"

"I don't get it," Ty said.

"That's what we were hearing. We just thought he was saying Mister Ken, but he was giving himself a hard time for screwing up while practicing."

Mr. Thursday blushed above his beard. "It's a bad habit of mine," he said.

"It just sounded like 'Mister Ken,'" said Charlie.

"I have to practice every day, or otherwise I get rusty," said Mr. Thursday. "I would have asked to use these things, but it was supposed to be a surprise."

"A surprise for what?" asked Tyler.

"For the magic show," said Mr. Thursday. "Of course."

The Final Mysteries

"Wait a second," Tyler said. "What magic show? I haven't heard about any magic show."

"A magic show like the ones the Abracadabra had in the old days," said Thursday. His voice was full of excitement. "And you haven't heard about it because it's a surprise," he added. "The magicians here are all organizing it."

"Wow!" said Tyler. "Mom will have to hear about all this. She'll love it!"

Mr. Thursday smiled. "Uh, you don't mind if I keep practicing, do you?" he asked.

"What? Oh, no, knock yourself out," said Tyler. "But it would be better if you used your own stuff, since it's here. Can you help me take these bowling pins back upstairs?"

"No problem," said Thursday.

* * *

Later, after Charlie, Tyler, and Mr. Thursday had returned the missing objects to their rightful places, Charlie stood in the lobby next to the front doors. It was still raining outside.

He stared at the tall painting of the former Abracadabra, the hotel's founder. He was studying the magician's eyes.

Tyler walked up to him. "Hey, you might want this," he said. He handed Charlie an umbrella. "People always forget theirs when they leave the hotel, so we have lots of extra ones around."

"Thanks," said Charlie.

"No problem," said Tyler. "Well, so it wasn't a ghost after all. And Mom won't deduct my money to pay for the stuff."

"Great," said Charlie.

"Well, see you at school," said Tyler. He started to walk away. But then he stopped and added, "Just don't talk to me there."

Charlie nodded and smiled. At school, he was the brain. Tyler was the bully. Everyone had their separate place at school. No one would ever suspect them of working together. But in the magicians' hotel, it was as if they became new people.

When Tyler had disappeared, Charlie hurried over to the row of elevators. He pushed the button. Just as he had hoped, the car on the far left opened.

"Going up, Master Hitchcock?" asked Brack.

The Penthouse

Charlie stepped briskly into the elevator. He watched his reflection in the shiny golden doors as they slid closed.

"This is where you saw the phantom of old Abracadabra, right?" asked Charlie.

"What's on your mind, young man?" asked the operator.

"Puzzles," said Charlie.

"More puzzles?" asked Brack.

Charlie nodded. "Someone stole the shower curtains from the other rooms on the ninth floor," he said.

"So I hear," said Brack.

"But it wasn't Mr. Thursday," Charlie said.

"Why not?" Brack asked.

"Why would he?" Charlie replied. "He only needed a dozen metal rings for practice. Besides, how would he get inside those rooms?"

"I'm not sure," Brack said.

"Someone who knew how to get the passkey could do it," Charlie said. "Someone who knew how to palm things."

"Ah," Brack said.

"Someone who could hang around the front desk and not be suspected," Charlie added. He looked up at Brack. "For example, like an old and very trusted employee, maybe?"

"Maybe," said Brack.

"And why would those other shower curtains be taken?" asked Charlie.

"Hmm," said Brack.

"Maybe to throw off suspicion from Mr. Thursday," Charlie said. "Because if his shower curtain was the only one that disappeared, people might investigate him."

"That could be true," Brack said.

"And if people investigated," Charlie said, "they might find Mr. Thursday in the basement, practicing. And that would spoil the surprise of the show."

"Perhaps," said Brack. "Perhaps you're right."

"Also, how would Thursday know where to practice his juggling?" Charlie went on. "This was his first time in the hotel. Only someone who knew the hotel like the back of his hand could tell him where to find a great rehearsal space."

"Could be," said Brack.

"And finally," said Charlie. "Who's the mysterious cleaner?"

"Cleaner?" asked Brack. "What do you mean?"

"The old theater," Charlie said. "The floor of the stage has been recently swept. Maybe mopped. It was shiny. It should have been dull and covered with dust."

"Why do you think that?" asked Brack.

Charlie shrugged. "Tyler said no one had been in the theater for years," he said. "So it shouldn't have been clean."

"I see," said Brack.

"If anyone had been in there," Charlie went on, "Tyler certainly would have heard about it. I mean, he hears about everything."

Brack smiled. "That's true," he said.

"And I even rubbed my hand along the back of one of the seats," Charlie said. "It was clean too. Someone was getting the theater ready for a show."

"Incredible," said Brack.

"And of course, I remembered certain things you said to me when Ty and me got off the elevator," said Charlie. "You said I had juggled the clues together. Mr. Thursday turned out to be a juggler."

"Isn't that interesting," said Brack.

Charlie nodded. "Then you said you hoped my solution to the ghost mystery would turn tragedy into comedy," he went on.

"Did I say that?" Brack asked.

"Yes," Charlie said. "The faces carved into the doors of the theater are the famous faces of Tragedy and Comedy. You can find them in lots of theaters. They're an old tradition."

"You know a lot of things, Master Hitchcock," said Brack.

"I read a lot," said Charlie. "And it helps that I have —"

"An acute visual memory," finished Brack.

"That's right," Charlie said.

He and Brack smiled at each other.

"You know a lot, too, Mr. Brack," said Charlie. "Your words to me in the elevator proved it. You knew what was going on all the time."

"I keep my ears and eyes open," said Brack.

"Someone is putting on a show," said Charlie. "Like the shows in the olden days."

"Is that so?" Brack said, a twinkle in his eye.

"Yes," Charlie said. "You know all about it. Thursday was invited to be part of it. Mr. Madagascar, up on the thirteenth floor, is planning on his comeback."

"So I've heard," Brack said.

"I'm guessing Mr. Madagascar is probably going to be in the magic show too," Charlie went on.

"Perhaps he is," Brack said.

"And who better to plan a magic show like the old days than a magician from the old days?" Charlie said. "And who better from the old days than the greatest magician of them all?"

"Who indeed," Brack said.

"Abracadabra," Charlie said.

Brack smiled. "I think you would make a very good magician yourself, Master Hitchcock," he said. "How did you solve this mystery?"

"Lots of little things," said Charlie. "But I really started thinking about it when you told us you saw the ghost here in your elevator. I looked at where you pointed, at the shiny doors. I saw my reflection, and that's when I started to put the pieces together."

"Of course," said Brack. "I am impressed, Master Hitchcock."

"When you look at your reflection, you see a ghost from the past," Charlie said gently. "Abracadabra."

"Yes, yes," Brack said. He smiled.

He looked at his reflection and added, "It's the eyes. Hair turns gray and falls out, ears grow bigger, wrinkles attack your skin. But a person's eyes stay the same."

"Just like the painting," said Charlie.

"I could never leave the hotel," said Brack. "It's my home. And I feel protective of the other magicians here. We don't have many places left, magicians. Not the ones from the old days, anyway. So I decided on this new disguise, this new identity."

"And a new name," Charlie said.

Brack smiled. "Yes," he said.

"Brack is short for Abracadabra," said Charlie. "I guessed that, too."

"You guessed very well," said the magician. "And you seemed to have solved all the puzzles. Well done. So I guess this is for you."

Brack pulled a gold card from his uniform pocket and handed it to Charlie. Charlie looked down at it.

"Thank you, Mr. Abracadabra," said Charlie, holding the golden ticket.

"My pleasure, Master Hitchcock," said Brack.

The elevator's bell dinged. The elevator stopped. The doors slid open.

Beyond, Charlie saw the roof of the hotel.

Trees bloomed in concrete planters. Then Charlie saw the stone house with bright windows and towers that stood out against the rainclouds.

"Would you care for a cup of hot cocoa?" asked the magician.

"But who'll operate the elevators?" asked Charlie.

"It's all automatic," said Brack, smiling. "I don't think anyone will mind if the hotel's two puzzle masters take a short break."

Charlie opened his umbrella, and the magician and the boy walked toward the house.

ABOUT THE AUTHOR

MICHAEL DAHL grew up reading everything he could find about his hero Harry Houdini, and worked as a magician's assistant when he was a teenager. Even though he cannot disappear, he is very good at escaping things. Dahl has written the popular Library of Doom series, the Dragonblood books, and the Finnegan Zwake series. He currently lives in the Midwest in a haunted house.

ABOUT THE ILLUSTRATOR

LISA K. WEBER is an illustrator currently living in Oakland, California. She graduated from Parsons School of Design in 2000 and then began freelancing. Since then, she has completed many print, animation, and design projects, including graphic novelizations of classic literature, character and background designs for children's cartoons, and textiles for dog clothing.

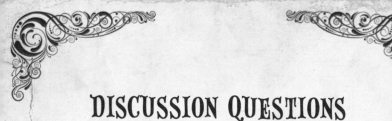

DISCUSSION QUESTIONS

1. Why did Brack change his identity?

2. Have you seen a magic show? Talk about some of the tricks you saw.

3. Would you want to stay at the Abracadabra Hotel? Why or why not?

WRITING PROMPTS

1. Try writing one of the chapters in this book from Brack's point of view. How does the story change? What does Brack see, hear, think, and feel?

2. Create your own magic trick. What is it? How does it work?

3. If you had to change your identity, who would you become? What would your name be, and what would you do? Write about your new identity!

GLOSSARY

acute (uh-KYOOT)—sharp

bizarre (bi-ZAR)—very strange or odd

circuit (SIR-kit)—a circular route

corridor (KOR-uh-dor)—a hallway

identity (eye-DEN-ti-tee)—your identity is who you are

investigate (in-VESS-tuh-gate)—find out as much as possible about something

orb (OHRB)—a circular object

phantom (FAN-tuhm)—a ghost

reputation (rep-yuh-TAY-shuhn)—your worth or character, as judged by other people

stickler (STIK-lur)—someone who insists on a certain level of quality

suspicion (suh-SPISH-uhn)—a thought or feeling

visual (VIZH-oo-uhl)—to do with seeing

MESSAGE FROM A GHOST

You can freak out your friends with this spooky trick. When your pet ghost sends you a creepy message, they'll be too scared to move!

You need: A shoebox, 2 sheets of paper, and a marker

PERFORMANCE:

1. Write a creepy message like "Boo!" on one sheet of paper. Crumple the message into a ball. Then place it into the shoebox with the blank sheet of paper. Keep the marker and cover of the shoebox in your magic box.

Message

2. Tell your friends you have a pet ghost and that it likes to leave you messages. Get out the shoebox and take out the blank sheet of paper. At the same time, secretly hide the crumpled ball in your hand as show

Message

Blank paper

3. Show that the paper is blank on both sides, then crumple it into a ball. As you crumple it, secretly switch it with the paper hidden in your hand. Then drop the message into the shoebox. Be sure to keep the blank paper hidden in your hand.

4. Next, get the marker and shoebox cover out of your magic box. When you reach in, drop the blank paper. Toss the marker into the shoebox and put on the cover. Then shake the box and pretend to wrestle with it as if your pet ghost was moving around inside.

5. Finally, remove the shoebox cover and take out the paper. Ask someone to open it and read it. Your friends will be amazed at the spooky message that has appeared!

MAGIC TIPS
Before doing this trick, try telling the audience a story about the ghost. Maybe you trapped it by the light of the full moon. Or maybe it's a friendly ghost that likes to help out with your magic show!

Like this trick? Learn more in the book *Amazing Magic Tricks: Expert Level* by Norm Barnhart! All images and text © 2009 Capstone Press. Used by permission.

WAIT!
DON'T FORGET!

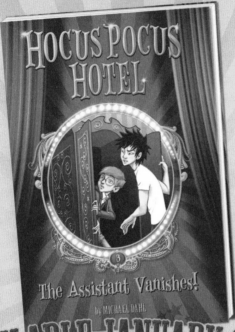

AVAILABLE JANUARY 2013!

FIND MORE:
GAMES, PUZZLES, HEROES, VILLAINS, AUTHORS, ILLUSTRATORS AT...

www.capstonekids.com

Still want MORE? Find cool websites and more books like this one at
www.Facthound.com. Just type in the Book ID 9781434241009
and you're ready to go!